To **Max**

For being good.
MERRY CHRISTMAS!

With lots of love

From   Granny Young xx

It was a crisp Christmas Eve
and Santa and his reindeers
were busy delivering presents to
all the good boys and girls.

Santa's sleigh zoomed over houses, twisting
and turning silently through the snowy night sky.
Santa squeezed down and up and up and down
chimneys, carefully and quietly delivering
lots of presents.

All was going to plan until he reached the second to last house on his list.

Suddenly, Santa noticed one of the presents was missing!

The reindeer looked in Santa's sack, they searched everywhere but the present was nowhere to be found! "Oh no!" exclaimed Santa. "It must have fallen off the sleigh!"

Santa **wondered** what to do.
He had no time to look for the present
but he didn't want to disappoint anyone
on his Christmas list.

Then
Santa had a
FANTASTIC
idea!

Naughty & Nice
LIST

He looked at his delivery map to see where they were.
Then he checked his list to see who had been **naughty** or nic

6

At the very top of the list was **Max**. So Santa and Blitzen (the smallest of all the reindeer) **squeezed** down the chimney...

his

into

bedroom.

quietly

crept

...and

MAX yawned, stretched and rubbed his eyes. He thought he was still **dreaming** until Blitzen licked his face with his long, wet, pink tongue - YUCK!

8

"I need your help!" boomed Santa.
He explained that a present had
fallen off the sleigh and
Santa wanted **Max**
to go with Blitzen
to find it.

Max of course was **VERY** happy to help.

9

It was cold and snowy outside so Max put on his warmest hat and long, stripy scarf.

Max and Blitzen looked through Santa's telescope.

They looked down past the houses and through the trees, trying to find the lost present.

Suddenly they spotted it, sitting on top of a pile of snow at the bottom of a big hill.

He jumped on Blitzen's back and gave him a friendly pat and little tickle behind his fluffy ears. Then with a gentle nudge they flew high into the starry night sky.

11

Up and up they soared and higher higher and higher

until Blitzen did a
loop the loop,
a flip and a flop
and landed with a bop
next to the pile of snow...

but the present had gone!

12

Max and Blitzen looked around but couldn't see the present **anywhere!**

All of a sudden Blitzen's wet nose began to twitch and itch and wibble and wobble. What had he found?

Max saw a bright orange carrot sticking out of the snow. "Who likes carrots?" he wondered. Perhaps this was a clue to where the present had gone.

13

Then they saw a tiny white and grey bunny rabbit

"Hello Mrs Rabbit, we're **looking** for a missing gift which fell from Santa's sleigh. Have you seen **anything**?"

The bunny **twitched** her nose, rubbed her ears and **pointed** a fluffy white paw at a line of acorns.

"Who likes acorns?"
wondered **Max**.

Then looking down, they noticed a
bouncy red squirrel staring back at them.
They followed him, picking up the **acorns** one by one,
not knowing who or what would be at the end of the trail.

15

As they picked up the final acorn, they noticed a nose-less, button-less, very sad SNOWMAN right in front of them.

His carrot nose had fallen off and his acorn buttons had been lost but there, poking out from under his black hat, was a shiny Christmas present!

16

Hurray, they had found the present...
but why did the snowman have it?

The sad snowman explained that every year he felt forgotten as he never received a present. When he found this one he was so **happy**. However, now he knew it belonged to someone else, he wanted to give it back.

Feeling sorry for the snowman,
Max decided to help.
He placed the half-eaten carrot
on the snowman's face for his nose
and the acorn buttons on his body –
but the snowman still looked sad.

Then Max
had a brilliant idea!

He undid his fluffy scarf and tied it around the surprised snowman.

Then he replaced the snowman's old black hat with his warm knitted one.

The snowman was so happy! At last he had his very OWN Christmas present!

Max and Blitzen flew as fast as they could to get the missing present back in time for Christmas morning.

Max placed the gift under the tree with a huge sigh of relief!

Back at home Max gave Blitzen a big hug, then watched as his new friend flew up into the sky and home to Santa.

When **Max** woke up on Christmas morning, he wondered if it had all been a dream. Then he looked out of his window...

...and there in the distance was the **happy** snowman waving at him and he was still wearing his **lovely** Christmas present.

The end